Disney · PIXAR

THE good, THE bad, AND THE robotic

By Dennis "Rocket" Shealy

A Random House PICTUREBACK® Book

 Published in the United States by Random House, Inc., New York, and simultaneously in Canada by Random House of Canada Limited, Toronto, in conjunction with Disney Enterprises, Inc.
Library of Congress Catalog Card Number: 00-108244
ISBN: 0-7364-1116-X
www.randomhouse.com/kids/disney www.disneybooks.com
Printed in the United States of America January 2001 10 9 8 7 6 5 4 3 2 1

Welcome,
future Space Rangers!
I know I make being
a defender of the galaxy
look easy, but it's not all
fun and games. Keeping
the universe safe is a
tough job!

If you think you've got what it takes, turn the pages to find out about some of the strange characters you'll meet. Luckily, the forces of good have plenty of backup!

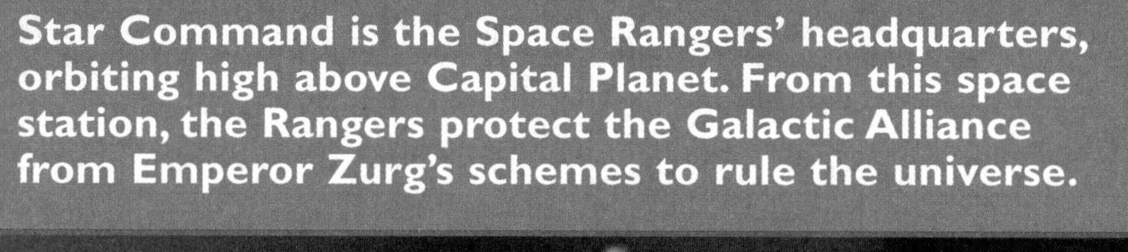

Star Command is the Space Rangers' headquarters, orbiting high above Capital Planet. From this space station, the Rangers protect the Galactic Alliance from Emperor Zurg's schemes to rule the universe.

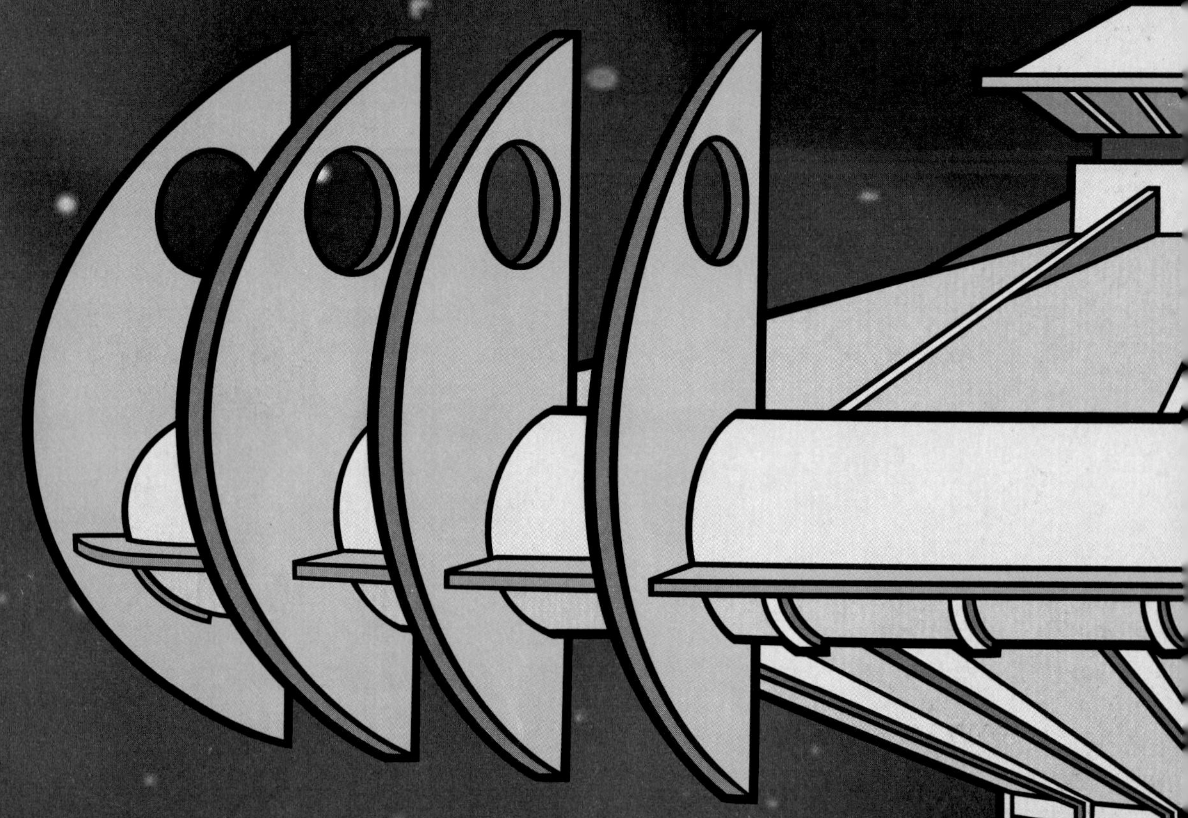

Run by the no-nonsense Commander Nebula, Star Command is always prepared to fight evil. The Rangers stay in shape in the training rooms and blast off into space aboard their space cruisers.

Mira Nova was a princess on the planet Tangea. Being a princess wasn't exciting enough for her, so she joined the Space Rangers. And she's become one of the best Rangers ever.

Mira Nova's ability to walk through solid objects and read minds has pulled the team out of the clutches of evil more than once.

She puts the *mira* in miraculous.

Booster Munchapper was a big boy who had big dreams. While growing up on the farming planet Jo-Ad, he planned to one day be a Space Ranger just like me.

It's like a cosmic Cinderella story come true. Except there's no glass slipper or prince or Fairy Godmother!

Booster worked his way up from Star Command janitor to full-time Ranger. It's now his job to press a lot of buttons and stare at stars on a tiny screen.

The Little Green Men, or LGMs, are the inventors and scientists aboard Star Command. They created the Space Ranger space suits and my robotic buddy, XR.

LGMs speak with one voice and act as one. That's because the Uni-Mind on their home planet links their minds together. When they're not on duty, LGMs like to hang out in the cafeteria.

They're small, they're green, and they like to build machines!

XR is an Experimental Ranger. The LGMs made him out of a collection of leftover gizmos. With an artificial intelligence chip for a brain, this metal man is ready to fight evil—but only when he absolutely, positively has to!

XR has been blown up many times in the line of duty. Luckily, the LGMs have always managed to put him back together to face new forms of evil.

XR is not afraid to run away from danger.

I was born to be a Space Ranger. I'm heroic and confident, and willing to soar to infinity and beyond in order to save the universe.
When I'm not fighting bad guys, I like to explore uncharted planets.

Buzz is my hero!

In my Space Ranger armor, I can battle anything. I can fly, shoot plasma blasts from my wrist, and survive in the airless vacuum of space.
I have defeated Emperor Zurg every time we have met in battle. As I often say, "There's no place for evil in this universe, even though it *is* really, really big!"

Enough about the
Space Rangers already!
Now turn the page to get
a taste of the evil side
of the galaxy.

Emperor Zurg has tried to take over the universe 3,247 times. And he has failed 3,247 times. But he keeps trying.

From his home, Planet Z, Zurg has come up with many evil plans, including turning the Rangers into jellylike blobs and building the most powerful weapon ever—the Evil Takeover Thingy!
Why can't everyone just fear and obey me like I want them to?

Warp Darkmatter is Zurg's henchman. Even though his space armor has been enhanced with extra evil, Warp is still no match for me.

Once, when a group of powerful aliens tried to capture me and Warp, we had to forget we were enemies and work together to escape.

What's the matter with this guy?!

The Hornets are Zurg's trusty helpers. These metal guys answer almost any command with "Obey Zurg!" They are always ready to do what Zurg wants, especially when he orders them to destroy Buzz Lightyear.

The Grubs also follow Emperor Zurg's orders, but they're really not bad guys. And that's why Zurg likes to use them as bowling pins when he's in the mood for a game of "evil bowling"!

Well, future Space Rangers, I think it's time we closed the book on evil. Good-bye and be good.
This can't be the last page! There's a lot more evil I want to let out! I deserve more pages! Or a book of my own!